Engineer Ari
and the
Hanukkah Mishap

For memories of Marsha, who collected friends wherever she went.

—D.B.C.

Text copyright © 2011 by Deborah Bodin Cohen
Illustrations © 2011 Shahar Kober
Photo p.32 by Garabad Krikorian, Armenian Patriarchate Collection

KAR-BEN PUBLISHING
A division of Lerner Publishing Group, Inc.
241 First Avenue North
Minneapolis, MN 55401 U.S.A.
1-800-4KARBEN

Website address: www.karben.com

Library of Congress Cataloging-in-Publication Data

Cohen, Deborah Bodin, 1968-
  Engineer Ari and the Hanukkah mishap / by Deborah Bodin Cohen ;
illustrated by Shahar Kober.
    p. cm.
  Summary: Near Palestine in the 1890s, a train derails and its
engineer, who was rushing to spend Hanukkah with friends, is
surprised when a Bedouin who helps him says they are in the very
place where the miracle of Hanukkah began.
  ISBN 978–0–7613–5145–0 (lib. bdg. : alk. paper)
  [1. Railroad trains--Fiction. 2. Hanukkah--Fiction. 3. Bedouins-
-Fiction. 4. Jews--Palestine--Fiction. 5. Palestine--History--1799-
1917--Fiction.] I. Kober, Shahar, ill. II. Title.
PZ7.C6623Emh 2011
[E]—dc22   2010016832

Manufactured in the United States of America
    1 — DP — 7/15/2011

GLOSSARY

Bedouins: nomadic tribe of Arabs

Dreidel: spinning top with four letters; The letters
on an Israeli dreidel stand for "A Great Miracle
Happened Here;" letters on other dreidels stand for
"A Great Miracle Happened There."

Hanukkiah: candelabra lit on each of the eight nights
of Hanukkah

Judah: leader of Maccabees

Sufganiyot: jelly donuts

Engineer Ari
and the
Hanukkah Mishap

By Deborah Bodin Cohen
Illustrations by Shahar Kober

KAR-BEN
PUBLISHING

Engineer Ari hurried through the bustling alleyways of Jerusalem, balancing an armload of packages. He held a crate of sufganiyot, a box of dreidels, and a bag of Turkish coins. A hanukkiah and a bottle of oil teetered at the very top.

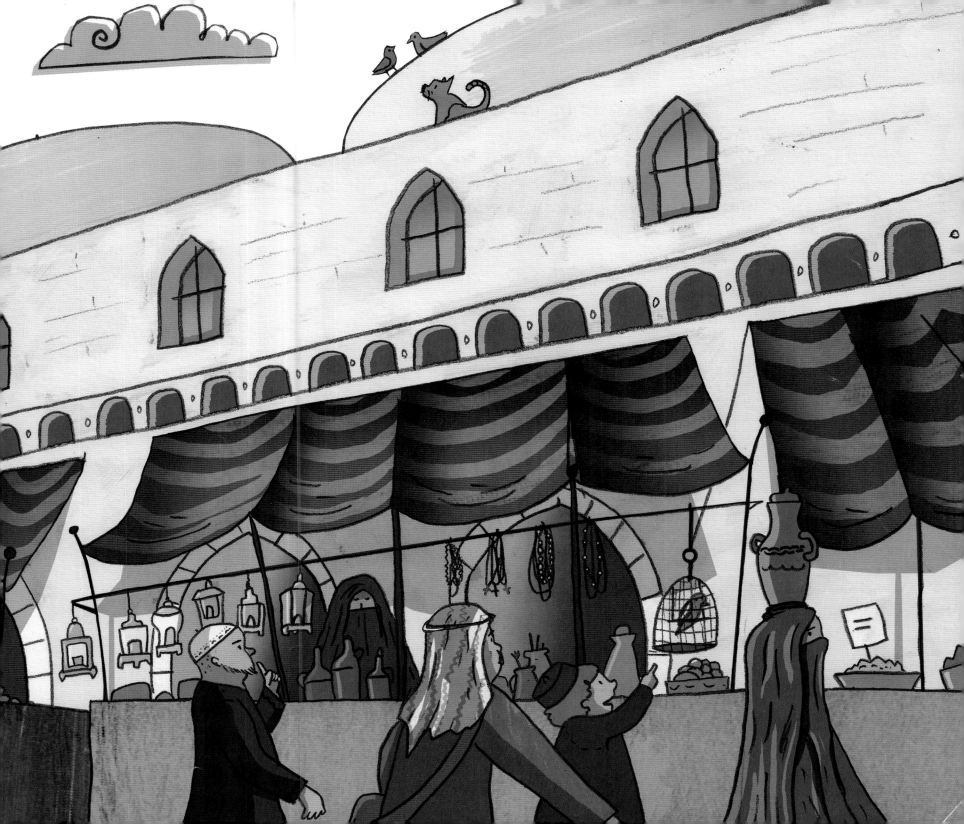

"Hanukkah starts in just a few hours," thought Ari. "I have barely enough time to take my train back to Jaffa and light the first candle with Jessie and Nathaniel." Ari and his engineer friends always celebrated Hanukkah together.

Making his way through the crowds, Engineer Ari saw two boys playing. One wore a crown, and the other held a shield. "Happy Hanukkah!" called Engineer Ari. "Tell me who you are."

"Mighty King Antiochus," replied the boy with the crown.

"Brave Judah Maccabee," answered the boy with the shield. "Long, long ago, I stood up to King Antiochus when his army captured the Holy Temple."

"His brave little army defeated our big one," added the boy with crown. "A great miracle happened here, right here in Jerusalem!"

Engineer Ari left the Old City through Zion Gate and followed the winding footpath toward the train station. As he climbed down and up, and up and down, his packages wobbled and he clutched them more tightly.

When he passed the new homes near Jerusalem's windmill, he waved to two girls playing dreidel under an olive tree. "Happy Hanukkah!" he called. "Can you tell me the letters on your dreidel?"

"*Nun, Gimel, Hay, and Pay,*" one of the girls called back. "That stands for *Nes Gadol Hayah Po* — a great miracle happened here, right here in Jerusalem!"

"When the Maccabees recaptured the Holy Temple, it was in ruins," the other girl continued. "They cleaned it until it sparkled, and relit the Temple's seven-branched menorah. They had only enough oil for one day, but those few drops lasted for eight days."

Ari continued to the station where he boarded his train and carefully stacked the packages behind him in the engine car.

"Toot!, Toot!"

He steamed out of the station, and soon the train was CHUG-a-LUGGING toward Jaffa.

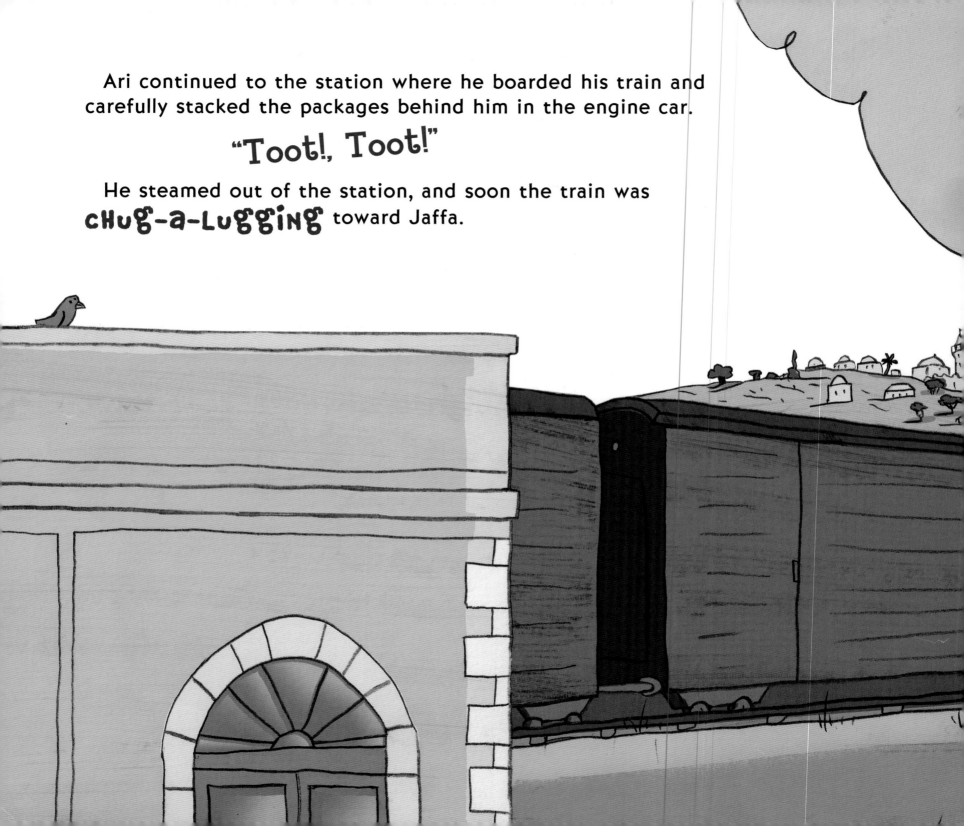

Ari imagined the smell of Nathaniel's delicious potato latkes and the sound of Jessie's beautiful voice singing the Hanukkah blessings.

Lost in daydreams, he drove his train around a bend too quickly.
"OH, NO!" he cried. A camel was sitting on the tracks! He slammed on
the brakes. **SCREECH! BANG! KABOOM!**

As the train squealed to a stop, Ari opened one eye, and then the other.
He let out a long sigh of relief. The train had stopped just in time. The
camel looked at Engineer Ari and bellowed a loud "**GARUMPH.**"

A Bedouin with long robes and a shepherd's staff ran up to the train. His son followed behind. "Oh dear, oh my, are you injured?" he asked. "My silly, stubborn camel would not budge."

"I am fine," said Engineer Ari. "But I fear my train is not."

Engineer Ari and the Bedouin inspected the train. The caboose had jumped the tracks. Ari's stack of Hanukkah packages had toppled to the ground and scattered.

"Your camel may be stubborn, but I was not careful," said Ari.

"My name is Kalil. Kalil means friend in Arabic," said the Bedouin. "Let me be your friend. You and I will pick up your belongings. My son will ride our no-good camel to Jaffa for help, and you must stay with me until it arrives."

"My name is Ari," replied Engineer Ari. "And I am most thankful."

Engineer Ari found his hanukkiah, a little bent, but not broken. The jug had tipped over and most of the oil had spilled out. "Like the Maccabees, I have oil for only one night," he thought.

Kalil shooed his goats away from the sufganiyot and picked up the scattered dreidels. Engineer Ari searched the ground for the Turkish coins. He picked up one, two, three coins, and then a dusty coin that did not look like the others. It was old and oddly shaped. A seven-branched menorah was engraved on its top.

"Look at this!" called Engineer Ari, showing the unusual coin to Kalil.

Kalil inspected it, "Have you heard of Modi'in?" he asked.

"The ancient home of the Maccabees?" Ari replied. "Where the miracle of Hanukkah began?"

"That's where we are!" said Kalil. "Long ago, the Maccabees lived on this very land, and you have found a Maccabean coin!"

Looking at the setting sun, he said, "Soon it will be dark. Come to my tent. I will make coffee while we wait for help."

"Kalil, Hanukkah begins tonight," said Engineer Ari. "Will you celebrate with me?"

"I would be honored," answered Kalil.

Once inside, Engineer Ari lit his hanukkiah and sang the blessings. He showed his new friend how to play dreidel, and together they ate sufganiyot.

Just as the oil burned low and the hanukkiah began to flicker, Engineer Ari heard a train whistle. He ran out of the tent.

"Toot!, Toot!"

Jessie and Nathaniel waved as their train CHUG-a-LUGGED up the hill and came to a stop. Kalil's son galloped alongside.

"Are you hurt?" asked Jessie.
"We were so worried," added Nathaniel.
Engineer Ari hugged his two friends and said, "I am safe.
I made a new friend. His name is Kalil. We celebrated Hanukkah
together on the very spot where the Maccabees once lived."
Miracles can still happen, they all agreed.

And to this, the camel bellowed a loud

"GARUMPH."

Author's Note

On August 27, 1892, the first train steamed into Jerusalem from Jaffa, carrying passengers and cargo. A month later, during the High Holidays, the railway officially opened. The train shortened the trip between the Mediterranean coast and Jerusalem from 3 days to 3½ hours. Eliezer Ben-Yehuda, the father of modern Hebrew, who lived in Jerusalem at the time, coined the word *rakevet* (train) from the Biblical word for "chariot."

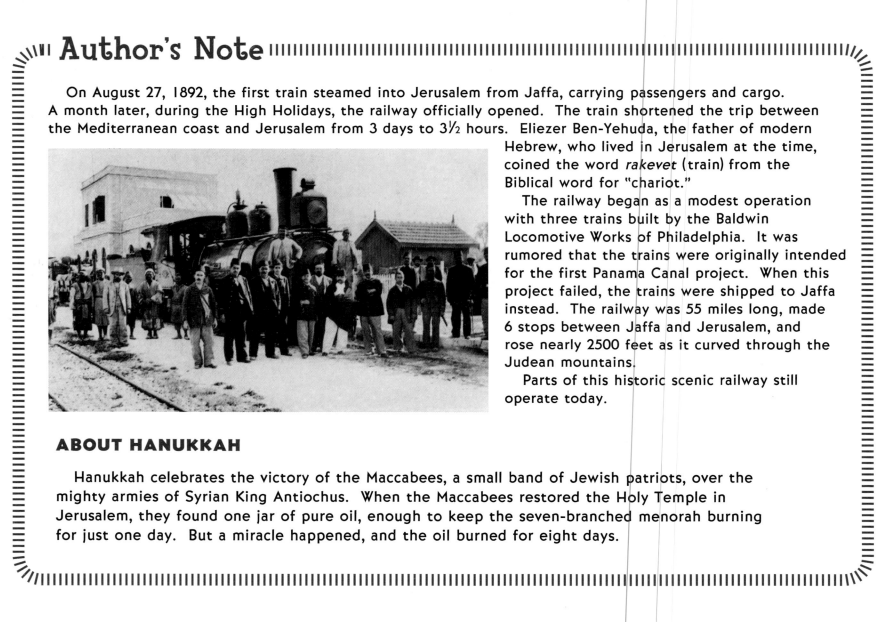

The railway began as a modest operation with three trains built by the Baldwin Locomotive Works of Philadelphia. It was rumored that the trains were originally intended for the first Panama Canal project. When this project failed, the trains were shipped to Jaffa instead. The railway was 55 miles long, made 6 stops between Jaffa and Jerusalem, and rose nearly 2500 feet as it curved through the Judean mountains.

Parts of this historic scenic railway still operate today.

ABOUT HANUKKAH

Hanukkah celebrates the victory of the Maccabees, a small band of Jewish patriots, over the mighty armies of Syrian King Antiochus. When the Maccabees restored the Holy Temple in Jerusalem, they found one jar of pure oil, enough to keep the seven-branched menorah burning for just one day. But a miracle happened, and the oil burned for eight days.